Señor Cat's Romance

and Other Favorite Stories
from Latin America

retold by
Lucía M. González

illustrated by
Lulu Delacre

SCHOLASTIC INC.
New York Toronto London Auckland Sydney
Mexico City New Delhi Hong Kong

ISBN 0-439-27863-5

Text copyright © 1997 by Lucía M. González.
Illustrations copyright © 1997 by Lulu Delacre.
All rights reserved.
Published by Scholastic Inc.
SCHOLASTIC and associated logos are trademarks and/or
registered trademarks of Scholastic Inc.

12 11 10 9 8 7 6 5 4 3 2   10   3 4 5 6 / 0

Printed in the U.S.A.

First Scholastic trade printing, July 2001

The poem, "Señor Cat's Romance," was
adapted from the Spanish by Melinda Munger.

Book design by Marijka Kostiw

The display type was set in Hadfield and Champers Plain.
The text Type was set in 15 pt. Cochin.
Lulu Delacre's artwork was rendered in watercolor
And gouache over cold-pressed Arches watercolor paper.

Special thanks to Teresa Mlawer for
reviewing the Spanish words and
fact-checking the manuscript.

Para mis niños,
Annie, José Antonio
y Mayarí
A la memoria de
mi hermana Malena

— L.M.G.

Para Lucas,
mi ahijado
y sobrino

— L.D.

Table of Contents

Foreword

The stories in this collection were first told to me by my great-aunt when I was still a child in Cuba. Now I live in the United States and have friends from all over the Americas. Whenever we speak about our childhood memories, it gives us great pleasure to discover that we sang many of the same songs, played many of the same games, and heard many of the same stories, even as we lived in different and distant countries.

These are stories that have spread beyond natural and political boundaries. They have become *"cuentos favoritos,"* or favorite tales, of children throughout Latin America. Some of these tales came with the Spaniards and other European settlers. Others came aboard slave ships from Africa and blended with the different indigenous cultures that were in the Americas for thousands of years. After countless retellings they have been adapted to the geographical and cultural environments of each country. These *cuentos* have become a part of the children's folklore of Hispanic America.

I read through many tales in published collections, both in Spanish and English, and I listened to many people from the different countries of Latin America as they told me the tales they knew. Then I selected those stories that were most widely known, and I retold the most popular versions.

The dominant themes of these stories are universal to the childhood experience. Their characters learn the power of sharing, they learn to overcome grief, they learn the value of wit and cleverness. These favorite traditional stories of yesteryear, now in English, will cross all boundaries of nation and language to enrich all of our children — today, and well into the future.

The Little Half-Chick

Once upon a time, a little half-chick named Medio-Pollito lived on a farm near the mill. He had only one wing and only one leg, and he did very well with these.

The other animals on the farm felt so sorry for him that they always gave in to his every whim. Because of this, he had grown to be a spoiled little chick who always demanded his own way, and nearly always got it. In fact, he was as naughty and vain as two whole chicks rolled into one.

One day he told his mother, "Mamá, I am tired of living on the same farm all my life. I am going to Madrid to meet the king! He will be very pleased to see me."

And off he went:

> *Tipi-Tap-Tipi-Tap-Tipi-Tap*

hopping on his only one leg.

On his way, Medio-Pollito came to a small brook. Its waters were choked with weeds.

"Medio-Pollito, help me!" coughed the brook. "Would you be so kind as to remove these weeds with your beak so that I may run free?"

9

But Medio-Pollito was in much too much of a hurry.

"I have no time to waste on anything so unimportant as water," said he. "I am going to Madrid to see the king!"

And he hurried away:

Tipi-Tap-Tipi-Tap-Tipi-Tap

hopping across the field on his only one leg.

Later on that day, he found a fire that was dying for lack of air. The fire gasped, "Medio-Pollito, fan me with your wing so that I may breathe and live."

But the little half-chick answered, "I have no time to waste on anything so unimportant as a fire! I am going to Madrid to see the king!"

And he hopped:

Tipi-Tap-Tipi-Tap-Tipi-Tap

a little faster on his only one leg.

At last, Medio-Pollito reached the outskirts of Madrid, from where he could see the palace gates. He grew so excited when he saw this that he hopped even faster. And as he rushed along, he passed by some bushes.

From among the branches came the voice of the wind calling, "Medio-Pollito, I am trapped in these branches. Please, come

10

and set me free!"

This time the little half-chick did not even stop as he replied, "I have no time to waste on anything so unimportant as the wind," said he. "I am going to Madrid to see the king!"

And he went on hopping:

Tipi-Tap-Tipi-Tap-Tipi-Tap

down the road that led to the palace.

In no time, Medio-Pollito arrived at the palace. He slipped quickly through the gates, past the guards, and found himself in a great courtyard. *Oh surely the king will be thrilled to see me now*, thought the little half-chick.

But just as he passed under the kitchen window, one of the royal cooks grabbed him!

"Just what I needed," said the cook. "A little chick for the king's soup!" And he threw Medio-Pollito into a big pot of water that was boiling over the kitchen fire.

As the water bubbled and rose, Medio-Pollito screamed, "Oh Water! Oh Water! My very good friend! Don't bubble, don't rise, or you'll drown me!"

But the water said simply, "You did not help me when I was in need." And the water went right on bubbling.

The fire crackled and blazed

beneath the pot. Medio-Pollito yelled, "Oh Fire! Oh Fire! My very good friend! Have pity, have mercy, don't burn me!"

But the fire said, "You were not my friend when I was in need." And the fire went right on burning.

Just then, the king came and looked into the pot. All he saw was a half-burnt half-chick. He reached inside, grabbed Medio-Pollito by his only one leg, and tossed him out the window saying, "This half-chick is not fit for a king's meal!"

But before Medio-Pollito could hit the ground, the wind lifted him up, up, up, over the roofs of Madrid and over the trees. Medio-Pollito shouted, "Wind, oh Wind, my very good friend. Don't blow me, don't toss me, don't drop me! Just let me drift slowly down, before I hit the ground."

But the wind exclaimed, "You did not help me when I was in need!" And the wind went right on blowing.

Higher and higher he carried the frightened Medio-Pollito. Then, at last, he swooped him down from the clouds and planted him right on top of the mill near the little farm that was once the little half-chick's humble home.

There Medio-Pollito stands to this day. He has had plenty of time to think about how he did not help his friends when they were in need. To show them he is sorry, he stands on top of that mill, on his only one leg, with his only one wing, watching from which direction the wind blows. And this is the way he helps farmers and travelers by telling them what kind of day it is going to be.

SOMETHING ABOUT THE STORY

The story of Medio-Pollito, "The Little Half-Chick," is widely known in Spain and Latin America. As a child, I was always delighted by the story of this willful and adventurous little chick who, in spite of his many limitations, sets out to see the world and meet the king. In his quest, he learns a very important lesson the hard way, but he still grows up to become a very helpful and important half-chick.

GLOSSARY

Mamá (mah · MAH)....Mama

Medio-Pollito (MEH · dee · oh poh · LYEE · toh)....Little Half-Chick

Juan Bobo and the Three-Legged Pot

There was once a boy who was so thickheaded and so foolish that everyone called him Juan Bobo, or Foolish John. One day, his mother was preparing *arroz con pollo*, chicken with rice, and found that she didn't have a pot big enough to hold it.

"Juan," she said, "I need you to go up the hill to your grandmother's house and borrow a big pot for making *arroz con pollo*."

"But Mamá," Juan complained. "I am so tired, and it is so hot outside today. Please don't make me go."

"Don't be so lazy, Juan," said his mother. "I want you to go right away, and don't take too long."

When Juan got to his grandmother's house, he said

15

to her, "Mamá sent me to borrow a big pot for making *arroz con pollo.*"

His grandmother went to the kitchen and brought back a wonderful iron pot, the old-fashioned kind, with three little legs. Juan took the pot and balanced it on his shoulders and started to walk home.

Right away, he grew tired, for the iron pot was very heavy. He set it down on the ground and studied it a while. It was then that he noticed its three little feet.

"Look at you!" he said. "You have three feet. I have only two. You should be able to walk faster than I can. Why should *I* carry *you*?"

He placed the iron pot on its three legs on one side of the road and he stood on the other side.

"Now," he said, "I'll race you home. *One, two, three!*"

Down the hill Juan ran at full speed and soon he reached home.

But when his mother saw him arrive empty-handed, she asked, "What happened, Juan? Where is your grandmother's pot?"

"Isn't it here yet? Hasn't it arrived?" cried Juan.

"What?" asked his mother.

"The iron pot, of course," said Juan Bobo. "I raced it home down the hill. And with its extra leg — why, it should have been here long ago."

"¡Ay, Juan!" cried his mother. "Go back quickly and get that pot before someone finds it and takes it!"

Poor Juan had to go all the way up the hill again. There, in exactly the same place where he had left it, stood the iron pot, resting on its three little legs.

"So, here you stand, you lazy iron pot!" he shouted. "Are you or aren't you coming home with me?"

KA-POCK!

He kicked the pot with all his strength.

The pot overturned and began to roll:

Ping! Pang! Pung!

clunking and clattering loudly all the way down the hill.

"Wait! Wait!" he called. "I had not yet counted to three."

But the old pot rolled straight down the hill and got to Juan's house long before he arrived.

Juan was very tired that day from all that running. So you can imagine how pleased he was when he discovered that the pot had obeyed him after all!

SOMETHING ABOUT THE STORY

"Juan Bobo and the Three-Legged Pot" is part of an enormous cycle of folktales about Juan Bobo, or Foolish John, many of which are found wherever Spanish is spoken. These are stories that tell of the incredibly stupid adventures of a fool, who sometimes turns out to be not so stupid. His apparent stupidity may, in the end, show that he is uncannily clever, or perhaps he was simply fortunate enough to have good luck on his side. Sometimes it is difficult to distinguish between Juan Bobo and Pedro Malasartes or Pedro Urdemales (Clever Peter), popular in Venezuela and Colombia. In Puerto Rico, Juan Bobo is the most popular folk hero. He represents the humor, the innocence, and the wisdom of the country folk.

GLOSSARY

Arroz con pollo (ah · RROSS   KOHN   POH · lyoh)....A delicious
   Spanish dish made with rice and chicken

¡Ay! (AHYEE)....Oh!

Juan Bobo (HWAHN   BOH · boh)....Foolish John

Mamá (mah · MAH)....Mama

Ingredients

2½ lbs. skinless chicken pieces
2 limes
Adobo seasoning *
1 oz. salt pork, diced
2 oz. cured ham, diced
2 tbs. olive oil
4 garlic cloves, crushed
1 lg. onion, chopped
2 lg. green peppers,
   seeded and chopped
1 tomato, chopped

Arroz con pollo

stuffed Spanish olives
capers
3 cups long grain rice
3½ cups water
1½ cubes chicken broth
¼ cup tomato paste
2 envelopes Sasón
   seasoning*
½ cup fresh cilantro,
   chopped
salt and pepper
*Available in Spanish
   food markets

Coat chicken with lime juice and sprinkle it
generously with Adobo. Set in refrigerator over-
night. In a caldero or heavy kettle, brown pork
and ham in olive oil. Add garlic and chicken.
Reduce heat to moderate. Brown chicken pieces for 5-10
minutes. Remove chicken pieces. Add onion,
peppers, and tomato and saute until tender. Add
chicken, and olives and capers to taste. Add rice, water,
salt and broth cubes, tomato paste, Sasón, cilantro,
salt and pepper to taste. Cover. Heat on high. When water
boils, turn heat to low. Cook for 20 minutes. Turn rice
with wooden spoon. Keep covered on stove for 10-15
minutes more.

Enjoy with a green salad. —L.D.
¡Disfrute!

19

Martina, the Little Cockroach

Once upon a time there lived a very charming and very clean little cockroach named Martina. One day, as she was sweeping the entrance to her house, she found a gold coin. The little cockroach, *la cucarachita*, had never seen so much money in her entire life. So she began to think: *What shall I buy with this coin? Shall I buy candies?* Ay, *no, no. They would not last me long.*

Then she thought a little harder: *Shall I buy some jewels?* Ay, *no, no. They would call me vain.*

Then she thought and thought and thought longest and hardest of all. Suddenly she cried out, "I know! I will buy a box of perfumed powder!"

And so it was that Cucarachita Martina went to the store with her little gold coin and bought a very exquisite box of perfumed powder.

That evening, she sprinkled a little powder all over her little self. *Ummm.* How good she smelled. She put on her best little evening dress. And she sat outside by the entrance to her little house.

She had not been sitting there long when Mr. Cat, Señor Gato, passed by and said, "Cucarachita Martina, you look so beautiful today! Will you marry me?"

The little cockroach patted her hair into place. "Perhaps, if you tell me how you would sound at night," she said.

"*¡Miau...Miau...Miauuu!*" sang Señor Gato in his loveliest voice.

"*Ay,* no, no," said Martina. "That would frighten me. I could never marry you."

So poor Señor Gato stalked away, feeling very sad.

A little later, Mr. Rooster, Señor Gallo, came along.

"Cucarachita Martina, you look so beautiful today! Will you marry me?"

The little cockroach patted her hair into place. "Perhaps, if you tell me how you would sound at night."

Señor Gallo stretched his neck and sang very proudly, "*¡Qui-Qui-Ri-Quí!* Cock-A-Doodle-Doo!"

"*Ay,* no, no," said Martina. "That would frighten me. I could never marry you."

And very sadly, poor Señor Gallo strutted away.

Then came Mr. Toad, Señor Sapo.

"Cucarachita Martina," said Señor Sapo. "You look so beautiful today! Will you marry me?"

The little cockroach patted her hair into place. "Perhaps," said Martina. "But first you must tell me how you would sound at night."

Señor Sapo filled his lungs with air to let his best voice come out:

"*Crr-oak...Crr-oak...Crr-oak...*"

"*Ay,* no, no," said Martina. "That would frighten me! I could never marry you."

And Señor Sapo hopped away, also feeling very sad.

It was already getting late, and Martina was just about ready to go back inside her house when little Pérez the Mouse, Ratoncito Pérez, came by. He was very shy and a very polite little mouse. Upon seeing Martina, Ratoncito Pérez stopped, honored her with a deep bow, and

23

then said in his sweetest voice, "Cucarachita Martina, you look so beautiful today! Will you marry me?"

The little cockroach patted her hair into place. "Perhaps," said Martina. "If you will tell me how you sound at night."

Ratoncito Pérez whispered very softly:

"Choo-ee...Choo-ee...Choo-ee..."

The sound was like music to Martina's ears. She loved it so much that she married him the very next day.

One day, sometime after the wedding, Martina had to go to the market to buy spices for an onion soup she was cooking for supper. Before she left the house, she

24

told her husband, "Ratoncito Pérez, watch the soup and don't try to drink it until I get back."

That little mouse loved onion soup. And as soon as Cucarachita Martina had left, he ran to the kitchen, climbed on the edge of the pot, and tried to reach a golden onion that was floating in the soup. But, ¡ay! alas, his foot slipped, and — SPLASH! — he fell inside the pot! Poor Ratoncito Pérez.

When Cucarachita Martina came home that day, she looked all over the house for her little mouse. But when she found him floating in the soup with a broken tail and burnt-up fur, she cried as if her heart would break. And as nighttime came, she sat outside the entrance to her house weeping and singing:

Pérez the Mouse
Fell into the pot
And Martina the cockroach
Cries her heart out.

Cucarachita Martina's singing was so beautiful and so sad that soon word of Ratoncito's terrible accident reached the king. The king sent his wisest doctors right away. And before very long, they were able to make Ratoncito Pérez as good as new!

SOMETHING ABOUT THE STORY

The story of Cucarachita Martina is part of the children's folklore of most of the Hispanic-American countries. Its popularity is equal to that of "The Three Bears" or "Little Red Riding Hood." It came to the Americas from Spain, where there are other stories told about the adventurous Ratoncito Pérez and Cucarachita Martina.

Their most famous story, the one most widely known among the children of the Americas, is this one in which Ratoncito Pérez marries the beautiful Cucarachita Martina and the sad case of his fall into the pot. Another is the story in which the king's wise doctors bring Ratoncito back to good health again after his accident.

This is the way the story was told to me as a child in Cuba, where Ratoncito Pérez's favorite dish was onion soup.

GLOSSARY

¡Ay! (AHYEE)....Oh!

Cucarachita Martina (COO · cah · rah · CHEE · tah   mar · TEE · nah)....Martina,
    the Little Cockroach

¡Miau! (MEE · aow)....Meow!

¡Qui-Qui-Ri-Quí! (kee kee ree KEE)....Cock-A-Doodle-Doo!

Ratoncito Pérez (RAH · tone · SEE · toh   PEH · rayz)....Pérez, the Little Mouse

Señor Gallo (say · NYOR   GAH · lyoh)....Mr. Rooster

Señor Gato (say · NYOR   GAH · toh)....Mr. Cat

Señor Sapo (say · NYOR   SAH · poh)....Mr. Toad

27

The Billy Goat and the Vegetable Garden

Once there was a very old woman and a very old man who lived on a farm. They shared a vegetable garden in which they grew tomatoes, lettuce, peppers, potatoes, beans, and plantains. They spent hours working in their garden and planning all the delicious dishes they were going to make with their vegetables.

One morning, a billy goat came into their garden and began eating up all the vegetables.

"Look!" cried the little old woman. "That billy goat is going to eat up everything in our garden. What shall we do?"

"Don't worry," said the little old man. "I can make him go away if I speak to him very, very nicely."

So he went down to the field where the billy goat was eating and he patted it on its back. "*Buenos días*, Señor Billy Goat," he said. "Good morning. Please do not eat up our garden. You are so young and strong, and we are so old and weak. Surely you can find food somewhere

else. Please go away."

But before the old man finished talking, the rude Señor Billy Goat's legs swung up in the air and his head bent low. Then he turned and charged at the old man with his horns!

"*¡Ay, Mujer! ¡Mujer!*" the old man cried out to his wife, running up the hill as fast as he could. "Open the door, please! The billy goat is after me!"

The little old man ran inside the house, shut the door, and began to cry.

"Do not cry," said his wife. "Perhaps a little tact and style is what he needs. I will go to him and make him go away." So she went down the hill to the field to have a talk with the billy goat herself.

Quietly, she tiptoed to where the billy goat was eating. Bowing low, she whispered, "*Buenos días*, Señor Billy Goat. A gracious good morning to you, kind sir, and I am sorry to disturb your breakfast. This fine food you are eating must have taken some poor farmer a long, long time and much hard work to till the soil, and to plant the seeds, and to pull the weeds. But now, I have come to ask you —"

That was as far as she got, for the billy goat

tired of her chatter and turned upon her. His legs swung up in the air and his head was bent low and he charged at her with his horns.

The old woman ran. Up the hill she went, crying, "*Ay,* Husband! Open the door, please! The billy goat is after me!" And she, too, tumbled inside the little house.

As soon as she was safely inside, they both began to cry. For they had been as polite and tactful as anyone could ever be. But that mean-spirited billy goat still got the best of them. Then suddenly, something tickled the little old man's ear. He shook his head to get rid of it and, as he did, down dropped a little red ant.

"I have come to help you," said the little ant. "I can make Señor Billy Goat go away from your garden."

"*You?*" cried the little old woman. "You are so small, what can you do? How can *you* help *us?*"

"Just watch me," said the ant. "You are being too nice to that bully. I can speak to him in the only language he understands."

And with that, the little ant crawled out of the house, through the field, and over to the billy goat. The goat didn't even

31

see the little ant as he crawled up his hind leg, across his back, straight up to his ear — and stung him!

"*¡Ay!*" cried the billy goat.

The little ant now crawled to the other ear and stung him.

"*¡Ay!*" cried the billy goat again.

Then the little ant crawled up his back and down again — stinging him all over as he crawled along!

"*¡Ay, ay, ay, ay, ay!*" the billy goat cried. "I have stepped in an anthill! If I don't get out of this garden at once, these ants will eat me alive!"

Quickly, he jumped up into the air and ran out of the garden as fast as he could.

The little old man and the little old woman gave many thanks to that brave and clever little red ant for saving their vegetable garden, and they always made sure he had plenty to eat. They spent many hours that fall harvesting their beautiful ripe vegetables and talking about the delicious dishes they were going to prepare.

And what about that billy goat? Well, for all anyone knows, he hasn't gone near that vegetable garden to this very day!

32

SOMETHING ABOUT THE STORY

There are many variations to this story in which the awful and stubborn billy goat tramples over a garden or eats the vegetables. Sometimes it is told as a cumulative tale in which a number of animal characters try and fail to scare the billy goat away. Almost always, it is a tiny ant or an insignificant little bee that succeeds.

This Puerto Rican version of the story is based on Pura Belpré's retelling in *The Tiger and the Rabbit and Other Tales*. Children laugh at the silliness of the old man and the old woman's politeness when they try to convince the billy goat to go away.

GLOSSARY

¡Ay! (AHYEE)....Oh!

Buenos días (BWEH · nos   DEE · ahs)....Good morning

Mujer (moo · HAIR)....Woman or wife

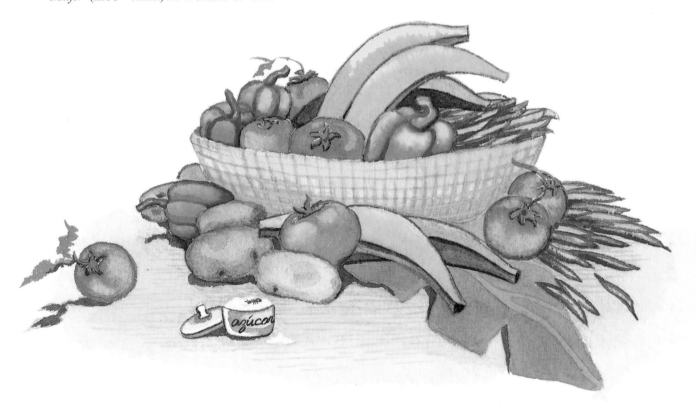

How Uncle Rabbit Tricked Uncle Tiger

Long, long ago, there were two good friends: Tío Conejo, Uncle Rabbit, and Tío Tigre, Uncle Tiger. Tío Conejo was very quick-witted and clever, too. He was always playing tricks on his friends — especially on his very nosy friend, Tío Tigre.

One day, Tío Conejo was resting under a *guamo* tree, eating a *guama* fruit that was as sweet and fluffy on the inside as cotton candy, when along came Tío Tigre.

"What are you eating, Tío Conejo?" said Tío Tigre as he sat down smiling and wagging his long tail from side to side.

Looking at the tiger's long, thick tail gave Tío Conejo an idea.

"*Ay*, Tío Tigre," said he, "don't you see that I'm eating my little tail?"

"Can you eat that?" said Tío Tigre.

Tío Conejo tried very hard to keep from smiling as he gave the tiger a taste of the sweet, fluffy guama he was eating.

"*Hummmm*, I love it!" said Tío Tigre, licking his whiskers. "Could I have some more?"

Now the rabbit had to try even harder to keep from laughing. "I would be delighted to give you more, but my tail is so small...."

Meanwhile, Tío Conejo could not take his eyes off Tío Tigre's long, spotted tail, which he wagged slowly from side to side as he sniffed around for more fruit.

"*Ay*, Tío Tigre," said the rabbit. "That tail of yours must taste very good! Look at it, so long and so thick!"

"Do you really think my tail would taste as good as yours inside?" he asked.

"Oh sure! The longer the tail, the better it tastes. But first we need to open it," said Tío Conejo.

"Would you help me do that?" asked Tío Tigre.

"Of course I will," said Tío Conejo. "Just turn around and hand me your tail."

So Tío Conejo got a good grip on Tío Tigre's tail and began to pull it, twist it, and turn it — until he had made a big, tight knot in his friend's tail.

Tío Tigre thought his tail felt funny, but he didn't know why.

Then Tío Conejo began to laugh, *"Hee hee hee hee hee."* He couldn't stop laughing as he told his good friend, *"Ay,* Tío Tigre, you sure look foolish with that big knot in your tail."

When Tío Tigre realized he had been tricked by his friend, he flew into a rage. He growled, and grumbled, and roared as he tried to catch Tío Conejo to give him a good beating. But Tío Conejo was very quick and had already disappeared into the bushes.

Poor Tío Tigre spent the entire night trying to untangle the knot from his tail. If he ever caught that rabbit, he would make him sorry he had ever thought of such a trick.

The following day, he decided to wait for Tío Conejo at the waterhole. Sooner or later, that rabbit would have to come for some water, and then he would catch him.

But Tío Conejo saw Tío Tigre hiding in the bushes.

For three days, Tío Tigre waited, and for three days, Tío Conejo couldn't have a drop of water to drink.

Tío Conejo could stand it no longer. He was so thirsty that he finally decided to go visit his friends the honeybees and borrow some honey from them.

He took the honey and poured it all over himself. After that, he rolled around on the ground under a tree. All the fallen leaves stuck to his honeyed fur. Then, all covered with leaves, he went to the waterhole and began to drink all that fresh, cool water.

Tío Tigre had never seen such a strange-looking little leafy animal at the waterhole. He was amazed to see how thirsty the little animal seemed to be.

"Little Leafy Animal," asked Tío Tigre, "when

was the last time you had any water to drink?"

Tío Conejo kept on drinking without even looking up.

Lapi-lapi-lapi-lapi.

Hmmm, thought Tío Tigre as he moved a little closer. "That little animal is either very hard of hearing or he doesn't want to speak to me."

"Little Leafy Animal," he said with a growl. "Can you hear me? When was the last time you had any water to drink?"

Tío Conejo continued to drink.

Lapi-lapi-lapi-lapi.

Now Tío Tigre was getting very angry. He could not believe how rude that little animal was. He moved right up behind him.

"Listen to me, *now,* Little Leafy Animal! I will not ask you again! When was the last time you had any water to drink?"

Lapi-lapi-lapi-lapi.

Tío Conejo finished drinking his water, wiped his whiskers, and then said, "Since the day I made that big knot in your tail, Tío Tigre."

Then he shook off the leaves from his body and quickly hopped away, disappearing into the thick, dark forest.

Since that day, Tío Tigre always chases Tío Conejo. But he has never, ever been able to catch him yet!

SOMETHING ABOUT THE STORY

Tío Conejo is a very clever and cunning little fellow who loves to play tricks on his powerful rivals, Tío Tigre (the tiger) or Tía Zorra (the fox), and always manages to get away with it. His power is not in his size, but in his genius. He makes children laugh and delights them with his ingenuity.

Stories about tricksters, *pícaros*, are favorites among the children of Latin America. The tales of Tío Conejo are most popular in places where there were large slave plantations. Anansi, the African trickster, and Brer Rabbit from the United States are his very close relatives.

The "tiger" in this story, Tío Tigre, is the Latin American counterpart of what is known in English as the jaguar. Although not as big as most tigers, he weighs about the same as a large human. His tail is thick and long and comes in very handy when he is balancing on tall trees.

This tale of how Tío Conejo tricks Tío Tigre by putting honey on his fur and disguising himself as a mound of leaves is one of their most widely told adventures. This is the way it was told to me in Venezuela.

GLOSSARY

¡Ay! (AHYEE)....Oh!

Guama (GWAH · mah)....Fruit of the *guamo* tree

Guamo (GWAH · moh)....A tall, branching tree with narrow leaves, planted to shade the coffee tree

Tío Conejo (TEE · oh   co · NEH · hoh)....Uncle Rabbit

Tío Tigre (TEE · oh   TEE · greh)....Uncle Tiger

Señor Cat's Romance

Señor Sir Cat, on his golden throne sat,
in Spain, once upon a time,
drinking spiced milk in his stockings of silk
and his golden shoes, oh, so fine.

A servant in livery brought a note, hand delivery,
what wonderful news he carried!
Cried Señor Sir Cat, "Ah ha! Look at that!
It says that I am to be married!"

His new bride to be — oh, so lovely was she —
a Moorish cat, rich and well-bred,
and a sight to behold in her dress of bright gold,
and her fur of the softest orange-red.

The very next day, in a church by the bay,
Sir Cat and his true love were wed.
They served nougats and sweets,
Spanish wines, and fine meats,
oh, their guests were most sumptuously fed!

"Let me sing of my love to the stars up above!"
sang Sir Cat from the roof where he'd climbed.
Oh, the joy that he felt made his happy heart melt —
but perhaps he took leave of his mind.

So happy was he caterwauling and howling,
and capering atop the church roof,
that too wildly he danced — and o'er the edge pranced —
hitting the ground with an *OOF!*

They called for the doctor, the surgeon, and barber,
who all said, "He cannot prevail!
He's crushed his poor paw and he's broken his jaw,
seven ribs and the tip of his tail!"

Next morning t'was time to bury the kind —
but foolish — Señor Sir Cat.
The Lady Cats wept, while the Tom Cats slept
wearing their black funeral hats.

The kittens wept sadly, their hearts broken badly,
"Miau-miau, miau-miau," they frowned.
But on each mouse's head, was a cap of bright red —
as *they* joyfully danced through the town.

In his coffin he rode, while friends solemnly strode,
in a line down the Alley of Fish.
But the sardines' aroma woke Sir Cat from his coma —
revived by his favorite dish!

When Sir Cat recovered, the mice he discovered,
and chased every one down the street.
Now it's no tale of wives — that cats have seven lives!
But for now, friends...our tale is complete!

SOMETHING ABOUT THE STORY

"Señor Cat's Romance" ("*El Romance de Don Gato*") is an old story from Spain. It is known as a song or as a story in rhyme. It is not usually played as a game. But sometimes, when the last stanza is, "*The mice run, run, run...and the cat runs after them!*" children will chase one another.

In Spain and Latin America, it is said that cats have only seven lives instead of nine.

Variants of this story are known in Argentina, Chile, Colombia, Venezuela, Ecuador, Mexico, Puerto Rico, Cuba, and in the United States.

GLOSSARY

Miau (MEE · aow)....Meow

Señor (say · NYOR)....Mister or sir

46